Writing this book was a lot of fun as I got to take over writing about Lewis from my dad. The idea for the story came from Homewood Suites. They help people and families whose homes are damaged because of large storms. They are always ready to lend a helping wing to those in need. Anyone can help after a storm, even you! Hope you enjoy!

"**O**h no!" cried Lewis the Duck. He and his wife Lois were home watching TV one evening when the weatherman suddenly appeared on the screen and warned that a huge storm was on the way. "Honey, why don't you phone the kids?" Lois asked. "Just to make sure they're okay." Lewis picked up his phone and called Lisa.

"Yes, Dad, Lance and I are fine," Lisa told him over the phone. "The storm is over already!" "Glad to hear it, Lisa," Lewis said. "Please stay safe, all right?" "We will, Dad!" Lisa replied. "Love you!" Lewis and Lois were thankful to hear that their ducklings were safe and sound.

T he pair awoke the next morning to find that the storm had made a huge mess of their house and neighborhood. "Oh Lewis, we need to get our house fixed!" Lois cried. "We will," Lewis told her, "but we need a place to stay while it gets repaired." He suddenly realized he knew exactly who to call.

L ewis dialed Jan from Homewood Suites by Hilton, a hotel for people who stay for long periods of time. Lewis wanted to see if there was a suite available while their house was being fixed. "Oh, I am so sorry to hear about your house, Lewis," Jan said. "But don't worry, we have plenty of room for you and your wife to nest."

ewis was excited to tell Lois the good news. "Oh, what a great idea, Lewis!" Lois cried happily. "It'll be like we never left home." They packed their bags and made it to Homewood Suites as fast as their wings could carry them. When they arrived, they found Jan waiting outside. "Welcome Mr. and Mrs. Duck! Make yourself at home!"

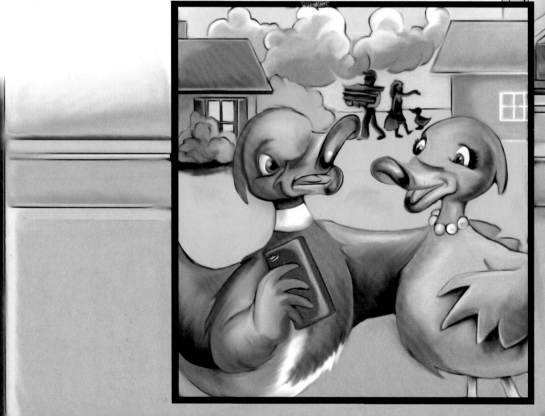

L ewis and Lois quickly settled into their suite. They unpacked then called a handyman to start working on their house. Jan brought them a welcome basket and made sure the Duck family had everything they needed.

That evening in the lobby, Lewis and Lois spoke with three other guests who were also staying while repairs were being done to their homes.

The first guest, Ron, was staying because his house was flooded. He went on to tell Lewis how the rain was so heavy during the storm that water poured in from the front and back doors. "I really hope it gets fixed soon!" he exclaimed.

T hen they met a young couple named Don and Jane who were staying with their three kids because the storm broke their windows and damaged the roof. "Oh, what a mess!" Jane cried. "I woke up the next morning to find broken glass on the floor and parts of my roof missing!"

J eremy, another guest, was staying because his house had no electricity. "My whole neighborhood was out of power, and we were told it may be weeks before it gets repaired. I need power for work!" Lewis wanted to help his new friends, but how?

Lewis saw Jan at the front desk and decided to get her help. After hearing Lewis's plan, she smiled. "Lewis! That's a great idea. The team and I were planning on cleaning up the neighborhood, so we'd be happy to help!" Lewis was excited; he was always ready to help his friends and community in a time of need.

The next morning, Jan introduced Lewis to her team and they went over the plan: host a supply drive, clean up the neighborhood and even visit patients at the local Duckville Memorial Hospital. The team knew what they had to do; now it was time to get going!

F or the first part of their project, Lewis and the team gathered
donations of food, clothing and supplies for people affected by the storm.
The drive was a success! People from all over town came to donate supplies.

N ext, they cleaned up the neighborhood. What a mess! Twigs and branches littered the yards and streets. Once they finished cleaning the roads and lawns, they all chipped in and helped Lewis' new friends repair their homes.

A s they were leaving, a team member noticed a small sad cat stuck high in a tree. "Oh, no! What do we do?" Lewis dialed the local Fire Department. "Of course, Lewis," the Fire Chief exclaimed. "We're on our way!" Soon, the team heard loud sirens and saw a large, bright red fire truck approaching. Help had arrived!

The firefighters used the large ladder on their truck to help Lewis get the small cat down. "Thank you so much for your help, Chief!" Lewis exclaimed. "No problem, Lewis!" the Fire Chief replied. "We're always happy to help!"

For their last project, Lewis and the team visited Duckville Memorial Hospital. What a surprise! The patients were happy to see Lewis and his friends from the hotel.

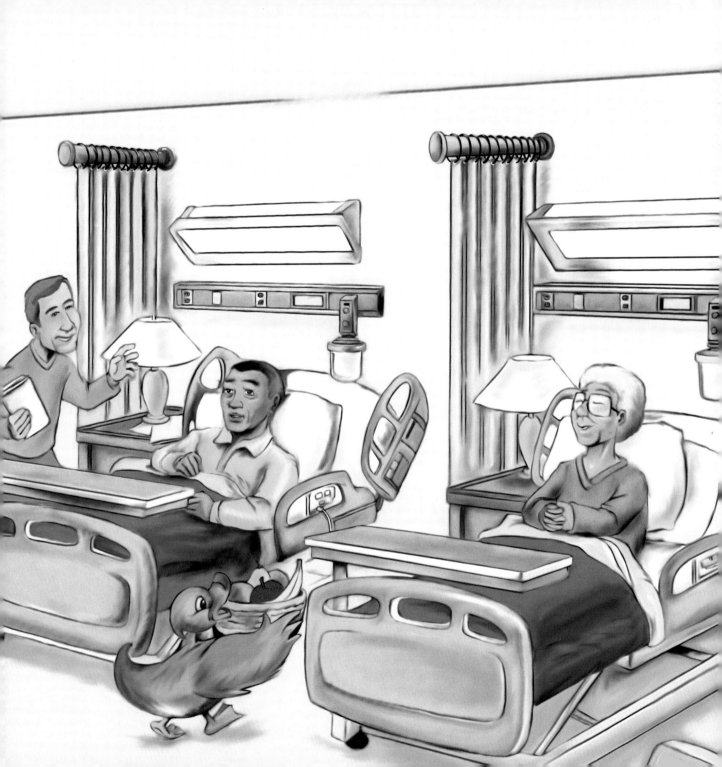

Lewis went to the Children's Wing and passed out games, books and toys for the kids to read and play with in their beds. Some of the children wanted to have their books read to them, and Lewis was happy to do so!

After several weeks of hard work, their projects were done. That night, the guests and some of the community members they had helped all held an appreciation party to celebrate the team's hard work. Lois gave her husband a huge hug. "I'm so proud of you, Lewis!" she exclaimed.

The next morning, Lewis got a call from the handyman who told him their house was finally ready. Lewis and Lois packed their things, said goodbye to their friends at Homewood Suites and took to the skies to fly back home. "Oh, Lewis!" cried Lois. "It looks as good as new!" "It really does." Lewis smiled. "It's nice to finally be home!"

That night, Lewis sat in his big armchair and began to think. He was very thankful that he and his friends were safe from the storm and things were back to normal. He also began to think about what he could do to prepare his family for the next big storm.

Author Bio:
Christian is no stranger to Lewis the Duck since this is his fourth book in the series. He joined his father, Bill, in writing *Lewis The Duck Goes to Mexico*, *Lewis the Duck Lends a Helping Wing*, and *Lewis the Duck Flies Around the World*. Christian lives in Memphis, TN, and attends Mississippi State University (Go Dawgs!).

Artist Bio:
Greg Cravens is the creator of the syndicated cartoon, *The Buckets*. This is his fifth venture with Lewis the Duck, as well. He enjoys spending time with his wife, Paula, and sons, Gideon and Cory.

The Story of
Lewis

Our guests often ask, "Why the duck?
Who is he and what does a duck have to do with Homewood Suites?"

Homewood Suites chose a duck because it symbolizes versatility and adaptability. Ducks are comfortable in air, in water, and on land. They migrate long distances over extended periods. And their ability to adapt and thrive in a variety of places represents our goal in the travel and hospitality industry — to serve guests with resourcefulness and flexibility.

We chose a wood duck, considered one of the most beautiful creatures in nature. And we've given him a name — Lewis. By naming Lewis and bringing him to life, we've created a visual representation of a unique brand that caters to those who want the comforts of home when on the road for a few days or more. And, with Lewis to guide us, there is no doubt that we will meet our guests' individual needs for comfort, flexibility and convenience.

HOMEWOOD
SUITES
BY HILTON®